How many
ducklings are in
the fountain?

Trampoline

Scooter

Pogo stick

Skateboard

Can you spot
the toy boat?

At the airport

How many planes
can you count?

Plane   Elevator   Belt loader   Baggage
x-ray   Baggage
carousel   Escalator

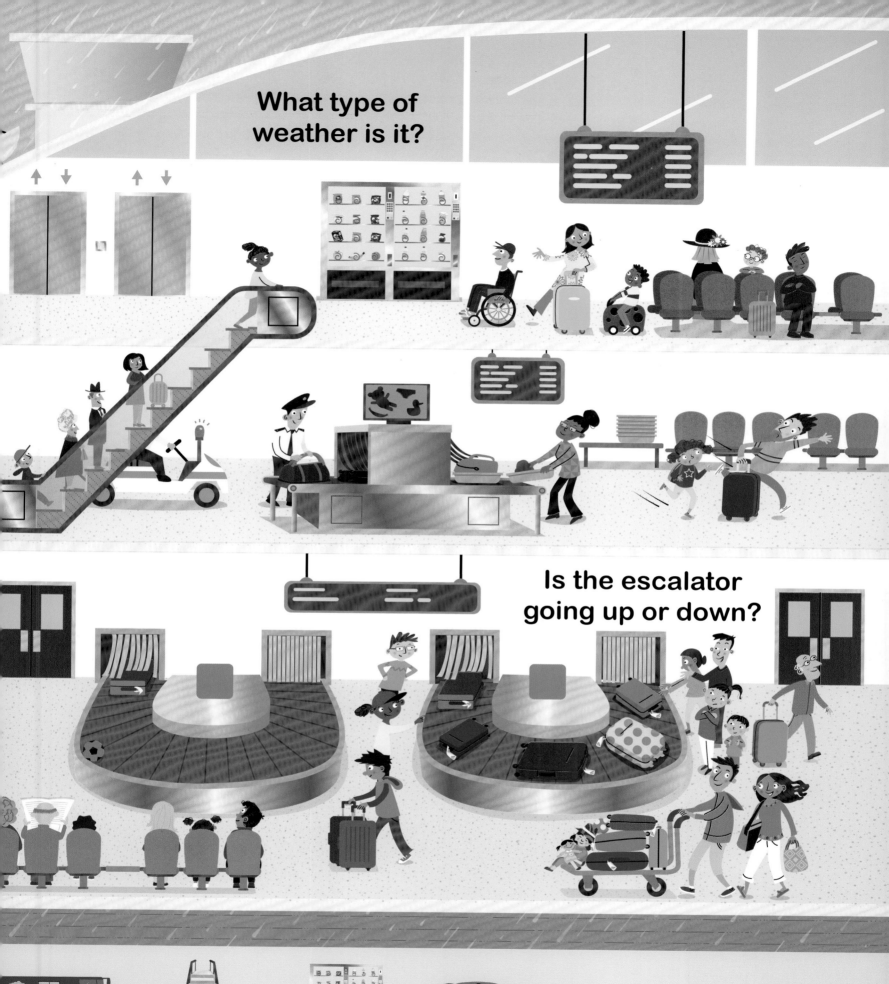

What type of weather is it?

Is the escalator going up or down?

Can you spot the electric vehicle?

Shuttle bus

Boarding stairs

Vending machine

Suitcase

At the seaside

What food is cold?

Surfboard

Lifeboat

Paddleboard

Paddle

Kayak

Speedboat

What animal is jumping out of the water?

Which boat is the biggest?

Can you spot the submarine?

Ship

Sailboat

Ice-cream cart

Fishing boat

In the mountains

Which skier is going to win the race?

Ski lift   Skis   Snowmobile   Rescue helicopter   Sled   Snowboard

How many dogs are pulling the sled?

What is the snowman wearing on its head?

Cable car   Ice skates   Snow shovel   Toboggan

Can you spot the skibob?

At the construction site

Which vehicle is red?

Bulldozer

Dump truck

Digger

Drill

Crane

Cement mixer

What do builders wear on their heads?

Steamroller

Road marker

Wheel loader

Forklift

Can you spot the jackhammer?

At the train station

How many people are on the bus?

Train **Bicycle** **Pedals** **Bus** **Streetcar/ tram** **Taxicab**

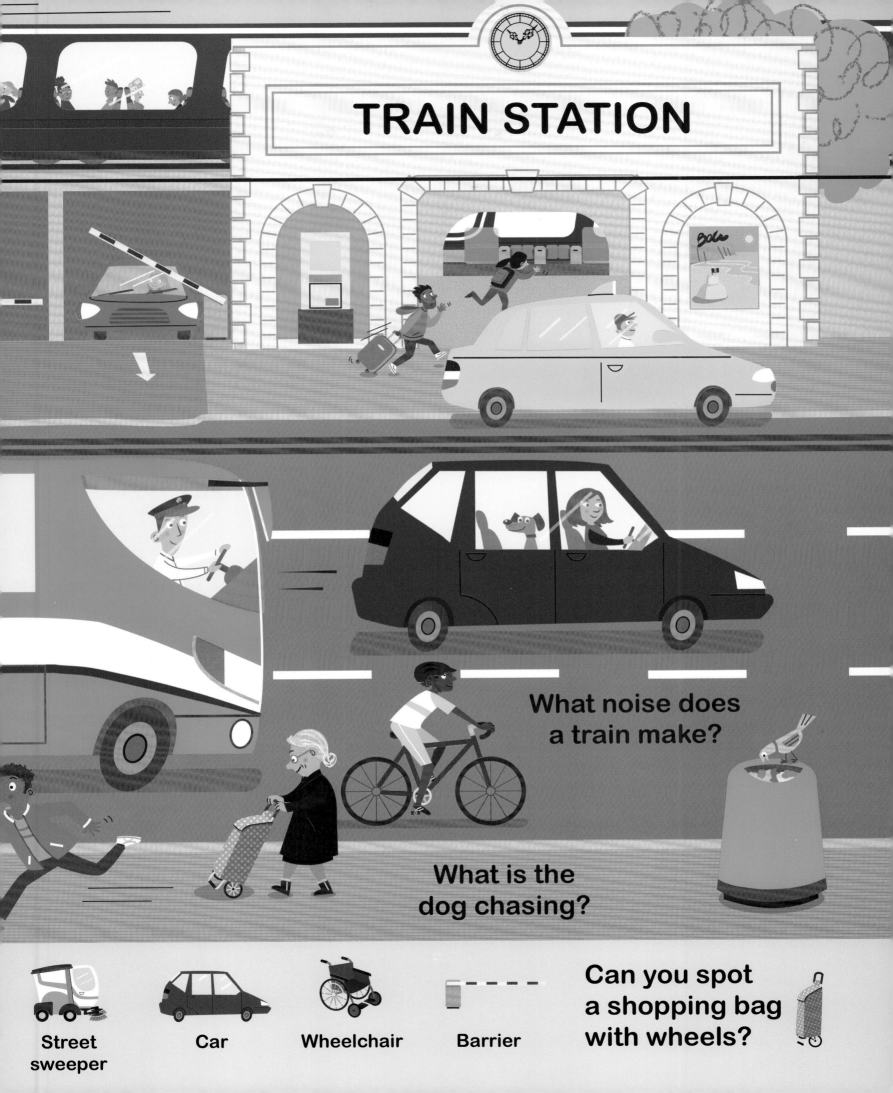

TRAIN STATION

What noise does a train make?

What is the dog chasing?

Can you spot a shopping bag with wheels?

Street sweeper

Car

Wheelchair

Barrier

At the amusement park

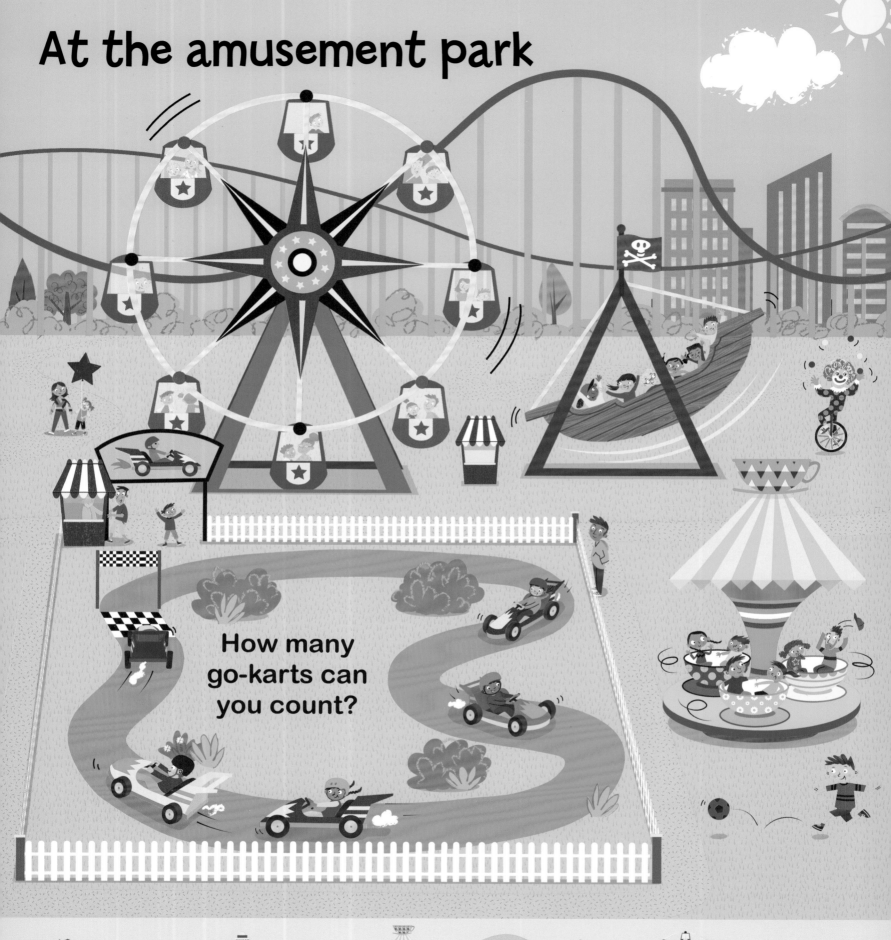

How many go-karts can you count?

Roller coaster

Merry-go-round

Teacup ride

Horse and carriage

Ferris wheel

Log flume

Who is juggling?

Can you spot the hot air balloon?

Go-karts

Pirate ship ride

Unicycle

Bowling alley

On the farm

Tractor

Trailer

Grain truck

Combine harvester

Potato planter

Can you name a vegetable?

What animal is in the trailer?

What noise does a sheep make?

Bale stacker

Wheel

Windmill

Hay baler

Can you spot the wheelbarrow?

At home

How many dogs can you spot?

Vacuum cleaner

Lawn mower

Stairlift

Treadmill

Cross trainer

Stroller

What is in the sky?

Where do you go to sleep?

Can you spot the toy car?

Tricycle

Clock

Fan

Handcart

On the street

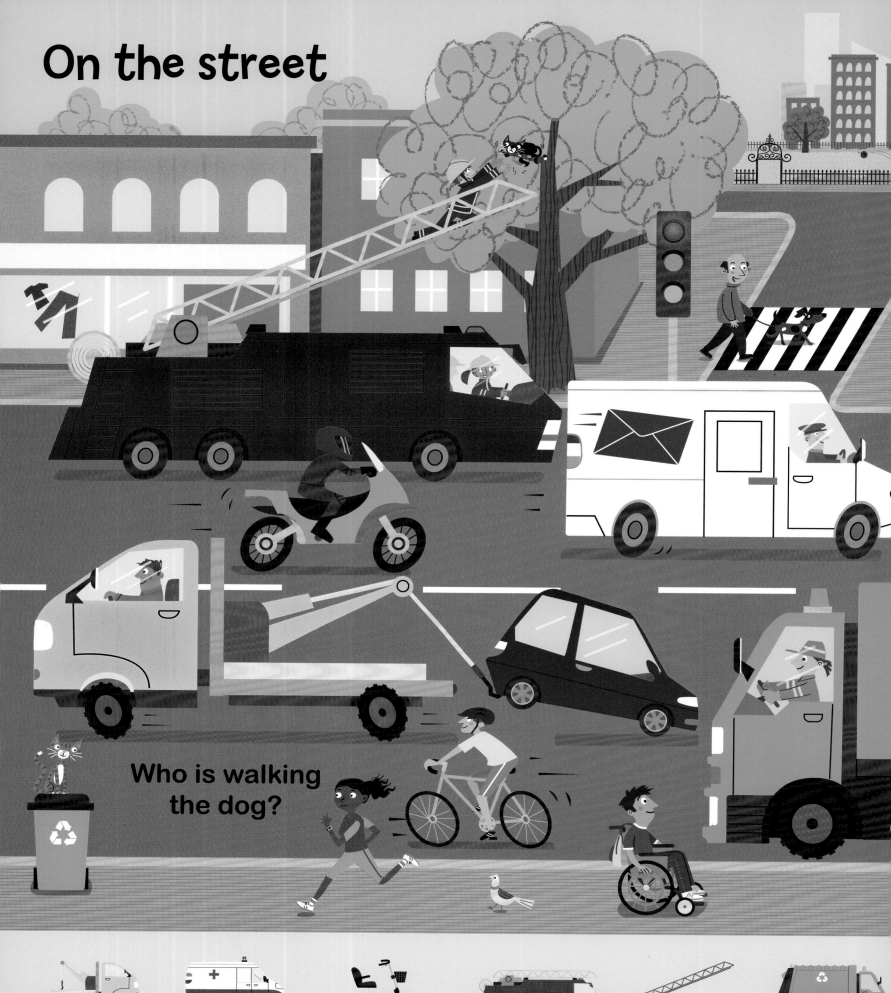

Who is walking the dog?

Tow truck

Ambulance

Mobility scooter

Fire truck

Ladder

Recycling truck

What noise does an ambulance make?

What animal is being rescued?

Police car

Motorcycle

Mail truck

Delivery van

Can you spot the siren?

In outer space

Where is
planet Earth?

Rocket   **Space shuttle**   **Lander**   **Rover**   **Satellite**   **Hoverboard**